JAN BRETT
The Hat

G. P. Putnam's Sons • New York

For Sara and Joshua Carty

Manufactured in China by South China Printing Co. Ltd.
Book design by Donna Mark. Text set in Bembo. Airbrush backgrounds by Joseph Hearne.
Library of Congress Cataloging-in-Publication Data. Brett, Jan, 1949– . The hat / Jan Brett. p. cm.
Summary: When Lisa hangs her woolen clothes in the sun to air them out for winter, the hedgehog,
to the amusement of the other animals, ends up wearing a stocking on his head.
[1. Hedgehogs—Fiction. 2. Animals—Fiction. 3. Clothing and dress—Fiction.]
I. Title. PZ7.B7559Hat 1997 [E]—dc21 96-54105 CIP AC ISBN 0-399-23101-3
11 13 15 17 19 20 18 16 14 12

Winter was on the way. Lisa took her woolen clothes out of the chest and carried them outside.

She was hanging them up in the fresh air, when a strong wind blew one of her stockings off the line.

Curious Hedgie found it and poked his nose in. When
he pulled it out, the stocking was stuck on his prickles.
"How embarrassing," Hedgie thought.

The mother hen came by with her chicks. "Cackle, cackle," she clucked, and laughed. "What's that on your head, Hedgie?"

"Why, it's my new hat," he told her. "Isn't it beautiful?"
The mother hen cocked her head as if she had an
idea. And off she ran.

Hedgie saw the noisy gander looking down at him.

"Honk, honk! Ho, ho, ho!" the gander laughed.

"Look at that! The hedgehog has flipped his gizzard."

"Laugh today, Gander. But tomorrow when it rains, my hat will keep me dry."

The gander thought for a moment. And off he ran.

The barn cat was watching from a tree as Hedgie tugged at the stocking.

"Meow," he called down. "What a silly-looking hedgehog you are, with that thing on your head."

"But my ears will be warm in a snowstorm."

"Hmmmmm," purred the cat. And off he ran.

The farm dog and her puppies found Hedgie in a patch of brambles.

"Hedgie, is that a hat you're wearing? How funny you look," she barked, and her puppies yelped and giggled.

"But I'll be cozy and dry when it snows,"
Hedgie said.

The farm dog's ears perked up. And off she ran.

"Oink, oink!" the piglets squealed.
"What are you up to, Hedgie?" the mama pig asked.

"Making sure my hat doesn't fall off if an icy
wind blows up."

"I see," said the mama pig. And off she ran.

"Hedgie, what is that ridiculous thing on your head?" the pony snorted at Hedgie. That was the last straw.

"It's my hat, of course. Don't you know that everyone should wear a hat in winter when it's cold and snowy!" Hedgie shouted.

The pony looked startled. Hedgie was usually so friendly. And off he ran.

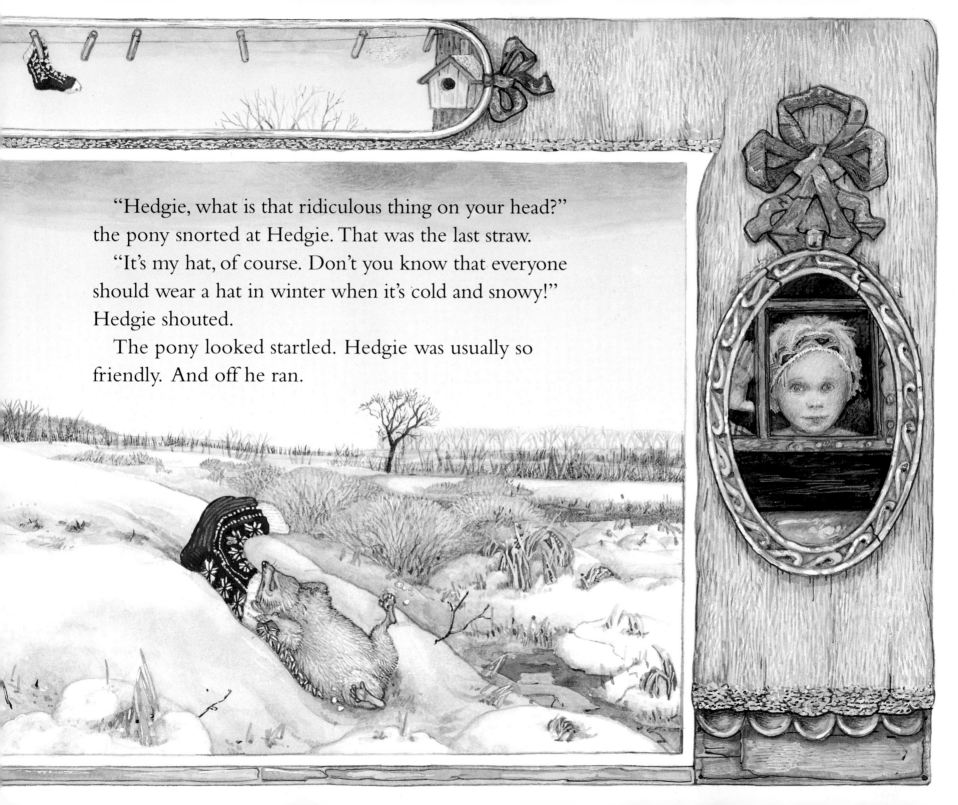

Hedgie just wanted to be alone. He was tired of everyone laughing at him, and with this thing on his head, he wouldn't even fit in his den.

He didn't see Lisa running after him, the other
stocking in her hand.

"Come back, you silly hedgehog," she called.

"Oh, no," Hedgie thought. "Even the girl is laughing
at me!"

Lisa caught up and pulled her stocking off
Hedgie's head.

"You ridiculous little hedgehog," she laughed.
"Don't you know that animals don't wear clothes!"

Hedgie headed for his den, and Lisa started back
toward the clothesline. That's when she saw all of her
missing woolens.

The animals had taken them and
each one was thinking, "Now *I* am
wearing a magnificent hat!"

Lisa was still chasing them when Hedgie reached his den.

"How ridiculous they look! Don't they know that animals should never wear clothes!"